06-100

John
and the
Fiddler

John
and the
Fiddler

by Patricia Foley
illustrated by Marcia Sewall

Harper & Row, Publishers

Typography by Patricia Tobin
10 9 8 7 6 5 4 3 2 1
First Edition

Library of Congress Cataloging-in-Publication Data
Foley, Patricia.
    John and the fiddler / by Patricia Foley ; illustrated by Marcia Sewall.
        p.   cm.
    Summary: A young boy befriends an old violin maker
who teaches him the beauty of music and friendship.
    ISBN 0-06-021841-X : $. — ISBN 0-06-021842-8 (lib. bdg.) : $
    [1. Violin—Fiction. 2. Friendship—Fiction.] I. Sewall,
Marcia, ill. II. Title.
PZ7.F734Jo 1990   89-34514
[E]—dc20   CIP
                                                                    AC

TO

Caitlin, Gillian, Bronwyn, and Caredwen

WITH LOVE

P.F.

TO

Milda S. Anesta

WITH APPRECIATION

M.S.

John
and the
Fiddler

I

John was sitting on the back porch steps clunking his heels against the risers. The big red dog lay at his feet waiting patiently for John to think of something for them to do. Every few minutes she made a small snorting noise that sounded to John like a sigh. It was a boring day. The same boring grass was poking up between the stones on the walk, the same boring bees were buzzing in the same boring raspberry bushes, and John figured it would probably be the same the next day. Bubber and his brother, Chip, the only other kids on the lane, were both away visiting an uncle, so not only was there nothing to do, there was nobody to do it with.

John's mother opened the screen door and popped her head out. "John, if you're not doing anything special, would you please bundle up my rocker in your wagon and take it down to Mr. McCleary and ask him if he can get out the squeak?" His mother attached a deal of importance to the rocker. Once it had belonged to her great-grandmother, who had been rather stout—which might have accounted for the squeak.

So John heaved himself up off the steps and went inside. He dragged the rocker out of the little room his mother used for sewing and lugged it down the narrow stairs, clunking it on the banister, and carried it out the kitchen door. He tipped it into his wagon. The big red dog came nosing over to see what was going on, and she and John went trundling off down the lane to Mr. McCleary's shop.

Mr. McCleary had lived in the village for as long as John—or John's mother, for that matter—could remember. His real name was

Sean MacLoegaire, but everyone called him John McCleary because that was easier to say and spell. He was, among other things, a fiddler.

He had a small shop in the barn out behind his house. There he made and repaired wooden things. He put new legs on old chairs, or recaned their seats. He built cradles for village babies and sanded the nicks out of pine tables that were beginning to show their age and glued up the joints of rockers that had rocked too many plump grandmothers.

He also made penny whistles and wooden flutes and fiddles—not to sell, but just to pass the time—and he had built John's wooden wagon especially so that John's Auntie Rin, who didn't have any children, could give it to John for Christmas.

In the dooryard the red dog twitched her floppy ears. Sean MacLoegaire was playing his fiddle. John pulled his wagon around to the back door and knocked. The music stopped.

11

"Come on in," said a crotchety voice from inside, "and don't let in every fly in the neighborhood!" Then the fiddle music started up again.

John took a deep breath and went in, closing the door quietly behind him. He stood in the kitchen holding on to the top rung of a ladderback chair while Mr. MacLoegaire sawed his way through to the end of the tune. Then he played the whole thing one more time, as fiddlers will. John stood patiently listening, and even tapped his toe a little in time to the music.

"Now, then," said Mr. MacLoegaire at last, waving the bow in John's direction. "What can I do for you?" He sounded a little gruff, but not unfriendly, and John began to feel less timid.

"Please, Mr. MacLoegaire," said John, "my mother's rocker is out in the dooryard with a squeak and she says can you fix it?"

Sean MacLoegaire put the violin on the thick pine table in the middle of the kitchen and turned a little screw at the end of the bow to loosen the horsehair. Then he stepped out of his slippers and into a pair of wooden shoes. John was a bit surprised. All the people he knew wore leather shoes. Mr. MacLoegaire said, "Who taught you to say my name that way—like an Irishman?"

"My Auntie Rin did, who gave me a wagon for Christmas. She said, 'That wagon came from Mr. MacLoegaire's shop and you'd better take good care of it!'"

"Your auntie wouldn't be the lady who runs the bakery, would she? There's a woman bakes a fine loaf of soda bread. And she's right about the wagon"—they were out in the dooryard now—"if it's made by hand, you must take especially good care of it."

Sean MacLoegaire lifted the little rocker out of the wagon and said, "Come on over to the shop and we'll see what needs to be done to this."

He opened the door of the shop and nodded to John to go in. The red dog was all set to follow, but Mr. MacLoegaire nodded to her to stay *out*, and she slunk off to sit by the wagon.

Mr. MacLoegaire set the chair down on the floor, pressed his hand heavily on the seat, and gave it a rock. *Skreak*, went the chair. "Rungs are shrunk. It's an old chair. The wood's dried out," he said. "If you want a good, tight chair, build it with legs that's a bit greenish and bone-dry rungs. The legs shrink as they dry and clamp right on to the rungs and you get no squeak. No squeak whatsoever. But I can fix this. You come and get it day after tomorrow.... Now, what are you gapin' at?"

John was not interested in chairs. John was interested in fiddles, and Mr. MacLoegaire's shop was full of them. There were all kinds of fiddles—some shaped like teardrops, some with wasp waists, like John's great-great grandmother (the one who had owned the rocker) in her corset and bustle before she got fat.

"Did you make all those?" asked John, pointing to the wall where the fiddles were hung between pegs.

"Oh, I did. Yessir," said Mr. MacLoegaire, "I love a good fiddle. Tell me, John—that's your name, isn't it? John? Same as mine, except mine's Sean, but it's the same thing. Do you like fiddles?"

"Yup. I have one, sort of. A make-believe one made out of a cigar box and a stick with rubber bands for strings. I haven't got a bow. I plink it with my fingers."

"Like a guitar, huh? Well, that's quite respectable." He was taking down a teardrop-shaped violin much smaller than the others. "I tell you what. We'll go back to the house and get my bow and you can have a whack at this. Can you imagine? I only got the one bow. I could make fiddles till the cows come home, but a bow is the dullest thing in the world."

And that's how John had his first violin lesson—on a teardrop fiddle, playing with Sean MacLoegaire's big old bow.

II

After that, John and the red dog went to visit Mr. MacLoegaire as often as they could. Sometimes John watched while the old man rushed or caned a chair seat. Sometimes he swept up shavings after Mr. MacLoegaire had worked the top or back of a violin with a little brass finger plane. Once, as he watched Mr. MacLoegaire carve a lion's head on the peg box of a violin, John said, "Who taught you to make fiddles, Mr. MacLoegaire? Your father?"

"Nope," said Mr. MacLoegaire, turning the peg head to one side to see if the lion still looked like a lion from the side. "My father was a fisherman. He drowned in a storm so long ago I can't even remember him. My uncle taught me. He was a carpenter, like me. He made fiddles for fun. Sold them at fairs and so on." Mr. MacLoegaire chuckled. "Times sure have changed. I don't suppose I could *give* these here away, never mind sell them."

"If I had some money," said John, "you could sell one to me."

Mr. MacLoegaire smiled. "That's very handsome of you, John, but I couldn't sell them anyway, any more than your father could sell you. The things you love you can only give away. You give them to the people you love. My big old violin, now...there's a thing I love. My uncle made it, and it came to me when he died. And when I'm dead and gone, that fiddle will go to someone I love— someone who'll love it as much as I do."

"Who's that?" asked John, feeling very curious and also a little jealous of this mysterious person Mr. MacLoegaire loved.

"Oh, never you mind about that," said Mr.

MacLoegaire. And then came the words John was always waiting for. "Get down the teardrop and let's have a tune."

So John tucked the teardrop fiddle against his shoulder and Mr. MacLoegaire settled his big old violin comfortably under his chin, and they began.

And this is how they did it. First Mr. MacLoegaire took the bow and played a little bit, and then sang the words, so it would be easier for John to remember.

When I was young, I had no sense.
Bought a fiddle for eighteen pence.
But the only thing that I could play
Was "Over the Hill and Very Far Away."

Then he handed the bow to John and said, "Now you try," and John played it after him.

III

One bright, windy day in early October, John and the red dog trotted into Mr. MacLoegaire's dooryard. John was just about to knock on the kitchen door when Mr. MacLoegaire's head popped out of the door of the workshop.

"I'm over here, John. Would you just step into the kitchen and get my fiddle and bow off the table and bring them over with you?"

John waved and nodded and went into the kitchen. A minute later he stepped into the workshop. There stood Mr. MacLoegaire holding something behind his back and smiling mysteriously. John held out the fiddle and bow, and Mr. MacLoegaire, still smiling his mysterious smile, held out his hand, too. In it was a violin bow—a brand new one, and much shorter than his own. It was just the right length for the teardrop fiddle.

Mr. MacLoegaire bent down and took his own bow and fiddle in one large hand. John just stood staring at the beautiful little bow. "Well?" said Mr. MacLoegaire. "Aren't you going to take it? It's yours, after all. What would I do with one that short?"

John took the bow and ran his fingers along the smooth stick. "You made it for me?" he asked wonderingly.

"I did. And what a chore. But you're getting to be a real fiddler now, and a real fiddler needs a bow of his own. The right size. And now we can play duets."

For just a moment John's throat felt too tight to let even one small word escape. Then, still holding his new bow, he flung one arm around Mr. MacLoegaire's neck and said, "Thank you."

Mr. MacLoegaire patted him on the back

and said, "You're quite welcome, John. Now, would you like to give that new bow a try?" He reached the teardrop fiddle down from the pegs that held it to the wall and handed it to John. Then he tucked his own violin into position and said, "How about 'Devil's Dream'?" And off they went. Of course, Mr. MacLoegaire made the fiddle sing and John made it squawk, but Mr. MacLoegaire didn't seem to mind, and to John it was all a great wonder.

So autumn passed, and the red and yellow leaves faded and fell from the trees, and Mr. MacLoegaire's fiddle sang and John's squawked, and the red dog lay in the dooryard and twitched her floppy ears.

IV

One morning, early in December, John jumped out of bed and looked out of his window. All the world was wrapped in a puffy white cloud. Thick snow was swirling around the house, and John couldn't even make out the copper fish weather vane on the roof of Mr. MacLoegaire's barn down the lane. "No school today," thought John as he hurried into his gray woolen pants and sweater and clumped downstairs for breakfast.

John's mother was in the kitchen paring apples and dropping slices of them into a pot of simmering oatmeal on the big black stove. She dropped a couple of curls of apple peel on the stove top and sprinkled a little cinnamon over them. John took a deep breath. The apple pie smell in the morning kitchen was the thing he liked best about winter, next to snow.

"Can I go over to Mr. MacLoegaire's after breakfast?" John asked his mother, who was stirring raisins into the steaming pot.

"Not today, John. That snow's deeper than your legs. You wait till the storm blows itself out and Dad and I get a path shoveled out to the lane."

John began to look very, very sad.

"And anyway," she continued, seeing how disappointed John was, "you wouldn't want to track snow all over Mr. McCleary's kitchen.... It's almost Christmas. Why don't you spend the day making Mr. McCleary a Christmas present?"

John perked up a little at the mention of Christmas, but not much. "What could I make him?" he asked.

"Well...I don't know.... You're a good

drawer, John. Why don't you make Mr. McCleary a picture?"

"What of?" grumbled John, but beginning to be a little bit interested, in spite of himself.

"Oh, I don't know. Whatever you think. It's supposed to be a present from you. He's *your* friend. Whatever you think he'd like a picture of." Then she plunked down a big brown bowl full of oatmeal and apples and raisins in front of him.

So John spent the day indoors at his desk, working with paper and watercolor paints to make a picture for Mr. MacLoegaire's Christmas present. By late afternoon, as the gray light closed in around the stone house, John's wastebasket was full of crumpled balls of damp paper, and his fingers were all the colors of the rainbow, but he was quite satisfied with himself.

He heard the cast-iron stove lid clatter in the kitchen. His mother must be poking up the fire. Soon she would begin cooking dinner. John blew on his picture to dry the last of

the wet paint and took it down to the kitchen. His mother was just removing two round, golden loaves from the oven.

"Well," John said, trying not to look *too* proud of himself as he held up the picture, "how do you like it?"

"It's wonderful, John. What a nice job you've done. Mr. McCleary will love it. I'll tell you what. You have just enough time before dinner to wrap it. I'll glue it onto a piece of cardboard for you so it won't get wrinkled. Then I'll get you some tissue paper, and you can color it and make it look pretty and wrap up the picture and put a ribbon on it."

So John took the battered fruitcake tin full of wax crayons from the bottom drawer in the kitchen cabinet, and his mother handed him a couple of sheets of white tissue paper. John drew Christmas trees and candy canes and snowmen all over the paper. Then he folded the paper all around the picture and stuck it up with a lot of tape. When he had finished, his mother gave him some red ribbon to tie around the package. Then she zipped the ribbon ends with her scissors and they turned magically into dancy little curls. John thought it was the best-looking Christmas present he had ever seen—especially the wrapping paper.

The next morning was bright and very cold, and as the sun climbed toward midmorning, the white birch trees at the edge of the woods behind John's house looked like slashes of chalk against the hard blue sky. Fresh snow was drifted over the lane and a brisk wind was whistling around the house, but John's mother said he might go down and look in on Mr. MacLoegaire and see how he had weathered the blizzard. So John, wrapped up in stocking cap and mittens and muffler, and the long-eared red dog set off down the freshly shoveled path to the lane and made their way through the drifts to Mr. MacLoegaire's. Ordinarily, John would have stopped to hit a few trees with snowballs or dived into the deep drifts by the side of the road. But today he had to take care of Mr. MacLoegaire's Christmas present, so he walked along like a grown-up through the shallowest parts of the drifts. His boots squeaked in the fresh snow.

V

Mr. MacLoegaire's house was just a whistle down the road, which was a good thing; otherwise the snowbanks might have tempted John sooner or later. But as it was, John and the present and the big red dog soon stood at Mr. MacLoegaire's house, blowing out puffs of steamy breath while they waited for Mr. MacLoegaire to answer the door.

Presently, they heard a cough and a croaky "Come on in and don't let all the warm air out. No use heatin' the whole outdoors!" John pressed the thumb latch and went in, nodding, in imitation of Mr. MacLoegaire, to the red dog to stay outside. She spotted some chickadees hopping about on the sparkling snow and took off after them.

"Hullo there, John," said Mr. MacLoegaire, who was sitting by the cook stove in a rocking chair with a brightly colored afghan tucked around his shoulders. John stared at the afghan—partly because it was so pretty, with dark brown and beige and cardinal-red and pine-green granny squares—and partly because it had a familiar look.

"Like this cover, do ya? Know who gave it to me?" asked Mr. MacLoegaire, looking tickled. "Your Auntie Rin, that's who. She's a corker. We're the oldest of friends, John. Did you know that? I believe we've known each other almost forever. She dropped by this morning with a loaf of soda bread and a jar of applesauce and a tin of good Irish tea and this here"—he stroked the afghan appreciatively—"all bundled up in strings and brown paper. 'Merry Christmas, Sean!' she said. 'Just thought I'd bring this around before the Christmas rush.'

"'And none too soon!' I told her. 'I got this

miserable throat. Can't catch a decent breath. Nothing for it but a cup of tea and a warm shawl by a hot stove.' So she brewed us a cup and didn't we have a good chat. I wish you'd have come earlier, John. You could have joined us."

It did sound cozy to John, who was sorry to have missed the tea party and his great-aunt, who was his favorite relative. But he was not unhappy, really, because it was good to have Mr. MacLoegaire all to himself.

"I brought you a present too, Mr. MacLoegaire. You can open it now, if you want, instead of waiting for Christmas. It might cheer you up and make you feel better." John handed him the package all done up in tissue paper and dangly, dancy ribbons.

Mr. MacLoegaire took the package in a hand that looked surprisingly young and nimble and said, "For me? Well, isn't this a day!" He unwrapped the package very carefully, so as not to tear the tissue paper, and held up the picture. He straightened his

arm and admired the gift from a number of angles.

"Well, now. Tell me: Did you paint this your own self?" John, a little embarrassed but very pleased at the excellent impression his gift had made, wriggled a bit and admitted that he had.

"Well, this is the finest picture I have ever owned. When I get over this sniffle and get my wind back I am gonna trot out to the shop and make me a frame for this paintin' and hang it right there"—he pointed to the wall opposite the rocker—"so I can look at it whenever I sit here roastin' my shins. Yessir, a very fine work of art. I like a man with an eye for the fine details. Look at them draw-knives, just the way I've got them hung in the shop, and you've drawn every hair on that foxy red beast of yours! I tell you what! This calls for a celebration. Go on over to the cupboard there and get us out that pot of apple-sauce, and that chunk of soda bread on the table, too." He got up, clearing his throat, and settled the afghan over the back of the chair. "We'll have our Christmas right now, on St. Nick's Day." He emptied a couple of generous tablespoons of tea from a green tin into the teapot and poured in boiling water from the kettle on the stove. Mr. MacLoegaire took two mugs down from a shelf beside the stove and filled them with tea. "Here you are, John. This will take the chill off. Help yourself to some of that bread." He sat down and wrapped himself up in the afghan. "Nothing I like better on a blastin' cold winter morning than a good, hot cup of tea. How about you?" And John agreed that there was nothing better.

"The only thing we want now is a bit of music. I'm a bit out of voice myself. Why don't you whip over to the shop and get the teardrop and your bow and bring them over and give us a bit of 'Jingle Bells'?"

So John got up, flung on his jacket without bothering to button it, since his mother wasn't around to scold, and dashed out to the barn to fetch the fiddle.

"Hear that wind!" said Mr. MacLoegaire as John kicked off his snowy boots. "Lay her over on the table for a bit, John. Let her get the feel of the kitchen while you finish your tea."

When John had finished his tea and licked the last of the applesauce and bread crumbs off of his fingers, Mr. MacLoegaire said, "You fetch me that fiddle and I'll tune her up for you and then I'll just pour myself another drop of this tea while you serenade me. Yessir, I call this the lap of luxury."

So Mr. MacLoegaire sipped his tea, and John, not sounding at all squeaky really, but rather nice, played "Jingle Bells" and "Deck the Halls" and "Brother John" and "Lady Mary Ann" and all the other songs that Mr. MacLoegaire had taught him during the turning and falling of the year. At first, Mr. MacLoegaire rocked and kept the beat with the toe of his slipper. But by and by he stopped tapping and rocked along dreamily

as if the music and the warmth of the stove and the soft afghan were lulling him to sleep.

"Well," said John at last, "I guess I'd better be getting home. Mother'll be wondering where I am and I s'pose you're tired out. Shall I put the fiddle back in the shop?"

Mr. MacLoegaire blinked in a startled way. "Going already? Well, your mother'll be thinking you've froze, I expect. Best set her mind at ease. And no, you shall not put that fiddle back in the shop. It's yours, from me to you, for Christmas. You just take that wad of brown paper over there on the table and wrap it up for the walk home." John just stared at him. Mr. MacLoegaire grinned. "What's the matter? Don't you want it?"

"Oh, yes! It's the thing I want most in the world. But I never thought I'd have a real fiddle. I promise I'll keep it forever and take real good care of it." He flung his arms around Mr. MacLoegaire's neck and hugged him. "Thank you," he whispered happily, not quite trusting his voice.

Mr. MacLoegaire chuckled and hugged him back. "Not at all, John. I'd always intended you should have it. What better occasion than Christmas? And I thank *you* for that picture. It's a humdinger!"

VI

Christmas Eve was bright with stars, and John, bundled in quilts, stared out his window into the night sky wondering where the end of it all was. Was there a stone wall somewhere out beyond the dark? And then what? When you climbed over it? More dark? More stars? He thought Mr. MacLoegaire might know, but he hadn't been allowed to visit Mr. MacLoegaire since St. Nicholas Day. His mother said Mr. MacLoegaire was down with pneumonia and was very, very sick and needed his rest, and no, he could not go visit. Pneumonia! John knew all about pneumonia. Pneumonia wasn't like an earache or something; sometimes people *died* of pneumonia. And Mr. MacLoegaire had it! That was when John began to worry. At first, it was just a small, nagging sort of worry—like a storm cloud a long way off. But the cloud seemed to draw nearer and nearer until finally it filled the whole sky and not even a shred of blue remained. But each time John begged to go visit Mr. MacLoegaire, his mother answered a bit more sharply, and with a wintry sort of look on her face that John had never seen before and didn't much like. So after a time, he stopped asking. But he didn't stop wondering or worrying, and a heavy feeling settled around him, a bulky sort of sadness that made him lonely and mopey and cross. Even playing his fiddle didn't help much. Holding it reminded him of Mr. MacLoegaire and how lonesome and worried he was.

Christmas was coming. His mother had made a large wreath of fir boughs and pinecones and cranberries for the front door, and

John had been allowed to take the step stool and a nail and hammer and hang it up. She made batches and batches of cookies and let him drop a bit of jam in the centers of some. Then he frosted gingerbread men to hang on the Christmas tree.

And he had gone into the woods with his father and the big red dog and cut down a great old fir tree festooned with a wild beard of dry moss. His father sawed off the very top and said, "That top will make a perfect Christmas tree, John. The rest we'll cut up and drag back for firewood. You'll have to string up an awful lot of popcorn to trim all these branches. We can put this fellow outdoors after New Year's so the birds can celebrate the holidays too."

And they had lifted the tree onto their toboggan and dragged it out, and the red dog had capered off ahead of them, stopping every now and then to burrow her nose in the snow. And in spite of it all, John still felt

heavy, and cross, and left out—and perfectly sure he would never see Mr. MacLoegaire again, even if the grown-ups couldn't quite bring themselves to say so.

VII

It was a swish and a whisper against the windowpane that woke John on Christmas morning. He poked his face out from under the warm quilts and said, "More snow!" Then he jumped out of bed and into his slippers and pattered downstairs.

In the parlor stood the tree, looking even more splendid than it had looked the afternoon before, when he and his mother had strung up the last of the popcorn and cranberry chains and his father had reached the harp-playing angel up to the very top of the tree. John thought the brightly wrapped packages scattered under the tree had been the missing ingredient.

"Good morning, John—and Merry Christmas!" said his mother, wiping her hands on her apron as she came in from the kitchen. "How late you've slept! Dad's gone for Auntie Rin, and if they haven't got lost in this squall they'll be here for breakfast and presents any minute. Go run up quick and put your clothes on."

John scampered back upstairs, yanked a red flannel shirt off the hook inside of his closet door, and dragged a pair of pants out of his drawer. In less than no time he was back downstairs. He had just finished washing up when his father and Auntie Rin came in the kitchen door, a freezing gust and a shower of snow blowing in with them.

"Merry Christmas, John!" said his father, shaking his snowy cap over John's head. "Look what the wind blew in!" John flung himself at his great-aunt.

She had her arms full of a large, bulky bundle, and she laughed her own jolly laugh

and said, "Heavens, John, you've almost bowled me over. Here, help me off with my rigging....I feel like a galleon in a gale." She set her bundle on the kitchen table. "Good grief, will you *look* at me? I'm an abominable snowwoman! Where shall I hang this stuff, John? Where do you put your wet mittens?" She hung her scarf around John's shoulders and pulled her crocheted hat down over his eyes and followed him into the pantry to hang up the snowy clothes.

"Jingle bells, jingle bells, jingle all the way..." she sang. "Do you know that song, John? Oh what fun it is to ride in a one-horse open sleigh!"

"Oh, sure, I know it," said John. "Mr. MacLoegaire even taught me it on the fiddle." Auntie Rin seemed suddenly very quiet, like a small bird when a hawk flies over, and the cold, lonesome feeling crept back over John again.

"What's the matter, Auntie?" he asked.

"It's only you've reminded me. I have to

tell you about Mr. MacLoegaire."

John stared at the toes of his shoes and Auntie Rin gave him a curious look.

Feeling like someone had just unscrewed the lid from a jar full of moths and now out they were fluttering, whether you wanted them to or not, John looked up and said, "He had pneumonia. And he didn't get better. They could've told me. I'm not a baby." He looked as if he might cry any second, and Auntie Rin seemed not to know what to say next.

They stood for a moment at the pantry door. Auntie Rin put her arm around his shoulders. Finally, she said, "He gave me a present for you and it won't wait one more minute, it's that important. Go on into the parlor. I'll bring it." She pulled a linen hankie out of her sleeve and gave her nose a loud blow.

"Open it," she said, "right away, before any of the other presents." She handed John a bundle and, to his surprise, sat right down

on the floor beside him. John turned the package over and began untying the string.

"Here, John," said his father, who had just come in with an armload of logs for the fire. "Just a second till I get rid of these....There, take my knife," and he handed John his jackknife.

John cut the strings and unrolled the brown paper. Underneath was the brown and beige and cardinal-red and pine-green afghan he had last seen tucked snugly around Mr. MacLoegaire's shoulders on St. Nicholas Day. There was something wrapped up inside it. Very carefully, John unwound the folds of wool. Inside were Mr. MacLoegaire's bow and fiddle. Around the neck of the fiddle was a tag, and the tag said:

TO JOHN—

FROM HIS FRIEND,
SEAN MacLOEGAIRE.

SOMETHING
TO GROW INTO.

Auntie Rin gathered up the afghan and drew it around them both, and for a moment they just sat there gazing at the fiddle. Then Auntie Rin smiled and said, "Do you s'pose you could give us a tune?"

About the Author

Patricia Foley was born in Philadelphia, Pennsylvania, and received her bachelor's degree in English from the University of Massachusetts. She now lives in Alexander, Maine, with her husband, John, and their four daughters. JOHN AND THE FIDDLER was originally written as a Christmas present for her daughters, all of whom play violins of various shapes and sizes. The details derive from Ms. Foley's experience as amateur musician and woodworker. JOHN AND THE FIDDLER is Ms. Foley's first book.

About the Illustrator

Marcia Sewall was born in Providence, Rhode Island, and now lives in Dorchester, Massachusetts. Inspired by her research for JOHN AND THE FIDDLER, she recently began taking fiddle lessons herself and can now play "Leather Britches" and "The Wind That Shakes the Barley."

Ms. Sewall has illustrated extensively, including three of her own books: THE PILGRIMS OF PLIMOUTH (Atheneum), ANIMAL SONG (Little, Brown), and THE COBBLER'S SONG (Dutton). In addition to eight books by Richard Kennedy, she has also illustrated THE BIRTHDAY TREE by Paul Fleischman; STONE FOX by John R. Gardiner; POOR BOY, RICH BOY by Clyde Robert Bulla; and THISTLE by Walter Wangerin, Jr.